Sarah & Duck

at the LIBRARY

Sarah and Duck set about their task.

1, 2, 3 . . . 4, 5, 6 . . .

Quack . . .

ack . . .

quack . . .

What are you two up to, then?

Counting the grass . . . to make sure it's all there.

Seems like you've counted quite a bit already.
How many do you have so far?

Mmmm . . .

Oh yes, and I think I might know where it's gone.

Donkey doesn't seem very sorry. In fact, he looks a little sad.

Looks like Donkey could do
with some cheering up.

Good idea, Sarah. A nice, crunchy carrot will cheer anyone up.

Donkey chomps down the carrot, but he still doesn't look happy.
What cheers you up, Sarah?

A cheerful tune on the tuba, maybe that will cheer Donkey up?

Maybe donkeys aren't fans of the tuba, Sarah?

Ah, perhaps a drawn-on smile might do the trick?

Oh look! It's landed on Duck's bottom!

Donkey **still** looks sad. What makes you happy, Duck?

A trip to the bread shop! Bread
will definitely make Duck happy,
and maybe it will cheer
Donkey up too?

Duck looks at all the golden breads in the window. It makes him very happy – **SO** happy he waddles straight inside!

That looks tasty, Duck.

Duck is happy, but Donkey still looks the same. I wonder what's wrong. Maybe we can look it up?

I know! The LIBRARY! They know about everything!

Of course! You'll definitely find a book about donkeys in the library.

Wow! Plenty of books here, but where to start . . .
Perhaps the librarian can help?

Maybe the farm section has books about donkeys?

Mmmm . . . over there!

Quack.

Oh look! Duck's found a book.

It's a tractor book, Duck!

says Sarah.

Quack.

says Duck, nodding.

Oh, it says, 'donkeys help dig fields with tractors,

but they can also be kept as pets . . .'

Aha! Maybe we should try the pet-book section?

The pet-book section is very **big**.

One of these books must be about donkeys . . .

Aha! Looks like Donkey
has spotted something.

It's a donkey book!
Clever Donkey!

says Sarah.

So, what does the book say?

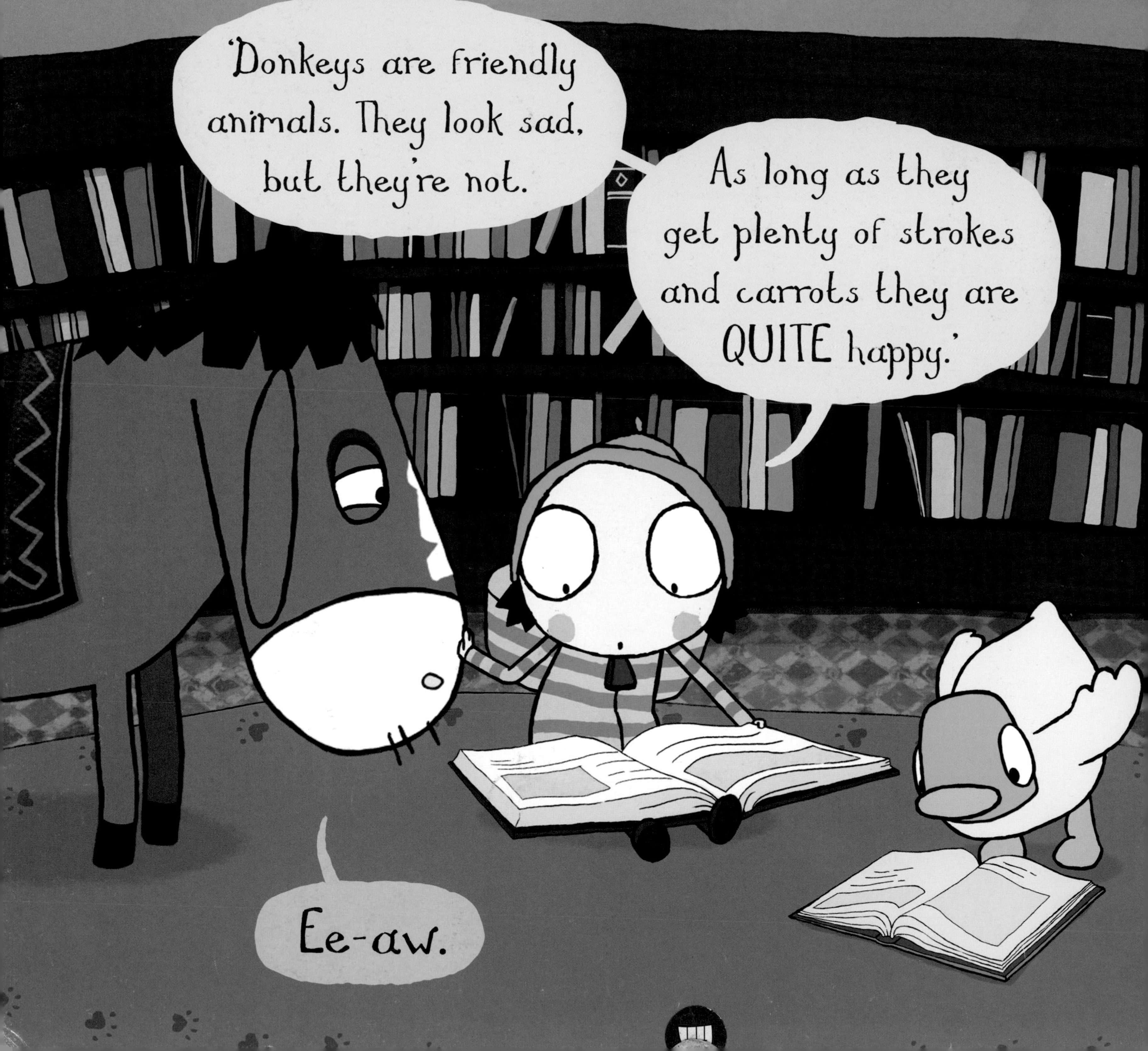

As they leave, Duck can't find his tractor book.

Sarah and Donkey are ready to go to the park, but it doesn't look like Duck is. He plods down the stairs slowly, and **very** grumpily.

Nothing like a good sit on the park bench. Now, how about some bread?

Quack. says Duck.

Oh dear. Now Duck doesn't look very happy.
What's wrong, chap?

Grumpy Duck! I know what'll cheer you up.

says Sarah.

Mmm . . .

What's that, Sarah?

The tractor book!

Well, that's certainly made Duck happy!

Oh look! Scarf Lady is back from the shops.

Hello!

Donkey looks happier than usual. Thank you for taking such good care of him.

says Scarf Lady.

Yeah. Well done!

says Bag.

Sarah gives Donkey a goodbye hug.

The End